FOR LIBBY

AND SUSAN

BARBARA ANN PORTE

Harry in Trouble

pictures by YOSSI ABOLAFIA

A YOUNG YEARLING BOOK

Published by
Dell Publishing
a division of
Bantam Doubleday Dell Publishing Group, Inc.
666 Fifth Avenue
New York, New York 10103

The trademark Yearling® is registered in the U.S. Patent and Trademark
Office.

The trademark Dell® is registered in the U.S. Patent and Trademark Office.

ISBN: 0-440-40370-7

Reprinted by arrangement with William Morrow & Company, Inc.,
on behalf of Greenwillow Books.

Printed in the United States of America

December 1990

10 9 8 7 6 5 4

WES

I, Harry, am in big trouble.

My library card has disappeared,
again.

"This is not the first time, Harry,"
I can just hear Ms. Katz say.

She is my librarian.

I don't know how to tell her.

"Something awful happened,"
I told Ms. Katz the first time.

"I was visiting my dog.
Her name is Girl.
She lives with my Aunt Rose
because my father is allergic.

"I had just come back from the library
with a stack of books.

"I put them on the kitchen table.
My library card was on top.
My aunt had just baked cookies.
They were on the table, too.

"'Have a cookie, Harry,' Aunt Rose said.
'Thank you,' I said.

"I ate one. Then I said,
'Have a cookie, Girl.'
I reached for one to give her.
That was when it happened.

"Girl jumped up to get the cookie,
my library card fell off the table,
and my dog ate them both."

"I see," said Ms. Katz.

"Is your dog okay?"

"Yes," I said. "She is fine,
  but I can't borrow books
  without a card."

"Yes, I know," Ms. Katz said.
  She made me a new one.

"Please don't feed this one
  to your dog," she told me.
"I won't," I said.
"I will keep it in my pocket,"
  which I did.

That is how
the second awful thing happened.

"Something awful happened,"
I told Ms. Katz that second time.
"Really, Harry," she said. "What?"

I said, "Remember my dog Girl,
who lives with my Aunt Rose?"
Ms. Katz nodded yes.
"Remember how she ate
    my library card by mistake?
Remember you gave me a new one
and said, 'Please don't feed this one
to your dog,' and I said—"
"Harry," Ms. Katz interrupted.
"Does this story have an end?"
"Yes," I said.

"I put my new card in the back pocket
of my blue pants.

"When my father
did the laundry on Sunday,
he put my pants in the washer
and dried them in the drier.

"When I put them on this morning,
my card was still in the pocket,
but now it isn't any good."

I held it out so she could see it.
"Please, can I have a new one?"

Ms. Katz sighed.

"That was a new one, Harry."

"Yes, I know," I said,

"but this time, I'll be really careful.
I'll put it in a very safe place,
I promise."

"I hope so, Harry," Ms. Katz said,
"because it's the last card
  I am giving you this year."
"Thank you," I said.

I put it in a very safe place.

Now I can't remember where.

I have looked in all my drawers,

in my closet, underneath my bed,

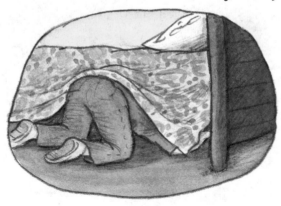

inside my books, and in my secret box,
which I keep hidden under my mattress.

I asked my father,

"Have you seen my library card?"

"No," he said.

I can't find it anyplace.

"I am in big trouble,"

I tell my friend Dorcas.

Dorcas moved here last month

from Ohio.

"My library card

has disappeared again."

Dorcas doesn't see the problem.

"A card's not so bad," she says.

"It's not as if you lost a book.

I lost three last year."

"Three cards?" I ask.

"Three books," she says.

"They belonged to my sister Sylvia.

You'd have thought I lost them

on purpose.

'If you'd learn to be more careful,'

Sylvia shouted at me in a mean voice,

'you wouldn't lose things

every time you turn around.'

"I am careful," Dorcas says,
"but I still lose things.

"Just since moving here
   I have lost a hat,
   two mittens—
   not from the same pair—
   my lunch ticket,
   and
   my brother Billy's baseball glove."

"What does your mother say?" I ask.
"She's used to me.

First she always says, 'Dorcas,

I wish you'd learn

to be more careful.'

Then she always says,

'When I was your age,

I lost things, too. I outgrew it,

and so will you.'"

"Your mother sounds nice," I say.

"Sure she is," Dorcas agrees.

"Isn't your mother nice, too?"

The hardest thing about new friends
is having to explain.
"My mom died when I was one year old.
She was in a car accident."
"I'm sorry," Dorcas says. "I didn't know."
Then she adds,
"I bet you had a swell mom, too."

That night I ask my father,
"Pop, when Mom was my age,
did she lose a lot of things?"

"I don't think so," he says.
"She was very organized.
   When she was your age,
   she told me,
   she made a card
   for every book she owned,
   and filed them in a drawer.
   She pretended she was a librarian.
   She insisted, for an entire year,
   that your Grandma and Grandpa Murray
   call her bedroom 'The Library.'"

"My mom was the best organized person
  in the world," I tell Aunt Rose
  the next day, after school.
"She never lost anything."

"I wouldn't know about that,"
says Aunt Rose.
"But I do know someone
who was always losing things."
"Who?" I ask.
"Your dad," she says.
I am surprised to hear this.
"Pop's so careful," I say.

"Sure, he's careful now.

Now he's grown-up.

But when he was your age,

our mother used to say, 'Sol-ly

(that was what she called him then),

it's a good thing

your head is attached,

or you'd come home without it.'

Sometimes he didn't come home.

He was lost, head and all.

"Your father loved parades.
He used to follow them.
He marched away with
fife and bugle sections,
clowns, and jugglers.
He was not particular.

"Usually he came home
in a police car.
An officer would ring the bell.

"Grandma would go to the door.
'Is this your little boy?'
the officer would ask."

"What did Grandma do?" I ask.

"She was always so glad
  to get him back,
  she'd hug and kiss him
  and warm up his dinner."
Aunt Rose smiles.

"I was always glad
  to get him back, too."

The next day, I tell Dorcas,
"When my father was my age,
he lost a thing or two.
What do you think
is the worst thing
that Ms. Katz can do?"

("No more library books for you,
Harry, ever," is what I think.)
"Send a note home to your father?"
Dorcas asks.
I think *that* wouldn't be so bad.
My father would probably just say,
"I wish you'd learn
  to be more careful, Harry."
Then he'd say,
"Don't worry, Harry.
  When I was your age,
  I lost things, too.
  I outgrew it, so will you."

Dorcas comes with me
when I go to tell Ms. Katz.

"I lost my library card," I say.

"Again," she says.

"Harry, it is not the first time
   this has happened."

I try to tell her that it is.
Once it was swallowed,
and once it was washed.
This is the first time
it was ever lost.
"Please, Harry," she says,
"I don't have time to listen now.
The question is,
what am I going to do about you?"

Dorcas and I wait while she thinks.

Finally, she says, "I am going
to make a new card for you,
but I will keep it at my desk.
When you want to borrow books,
you'll have to ask for it.
Does that sound fair to you?"
"Yes, Ms. Katz," I say.
"Then why don't you try to look
a little happier.
Let me see you smile,"
Ms. Katz says.

I smile, check out my books,
and give Ms. Katz my card.
Dorcas and I run all the way
to Aunt Rose's.

I tell her what happened.

Aunt Rose listens.

When I am finished, she says,

"Harry, your library card isn't lost.

"Don't you remember?
You needed someplace safe to keep it,
where Girl couldn't eat it,
and your father wouldn't wash it."
"Yes," I say, "but where?"

"You left it here, in my piano bench."

Aunt Rose goes into the living room.

Dorcas and I follow.

We watch as Aunt Rose lifts the top

of the bench

and takes out

my card.

"Wow," I say.

"Now I have two cards.

Won't Ms. Katz be surprised!"

Then Aunt Rose, Dorcas, and I
sit down on the bench
and take turns playing the piano.
We sing songs.
Girl sits next to us,
wagging her tail.
She points her nose up in the air
and sings along.